Library of Congress Cataloging in Publication Data
Krauze, Andrzej, 1947-
    What's so special about today?
    Summary: All the animals are on their best behavior
in anticipation of a big birthday party.
    [1. Animals—Fiction 2. Birthdays—Fiction]
I. Title.
PZ7.K8757Wh   1984   [E]   83-17499
ISBN 0-688-02835-7

Printed and bound in Italy by New Interlitho S.P.A., Milan,
for Sadie Fields Productions, Ltd., 866 United Nations Plaza,
Suite 4030, New York 10017.
First U.S. Edition
1 2 3 4 5 6 7 8 9 10

WHAT'S SO SPECIAL ABOUT TODAY?

PICTURES AND TEXT BY
ANDRZEJ KRAUZE

LOTHROP, LEE & SHEPARD BOOKS · NEW YORK

Why did T.T. Tortoise

leave home before dawn today?

Why did Granny Owl

spend all night baking a cake?

Why did Freddy Frog

press his best suit at dawn?

Why did Sarah Stork

polish her long beak this morning?

Why did Reggie Rabbit

pick his most beautiful roses today?

Why did Twiggy Piggy

spend all day in the bath?

Why did Colonel Cockerel

decide to wear all his medals today?

Why did Abner Turkey

choose today to share his best cider?

Why did Christopher Crocodile

work on his bicycle all afternoon?

Why did Ellie Elephant and her son Elmo

play a song until it was perfect?

AND why didn't Toby Dog

start a fight with Caroline Cat today?

Because . . . because . . .

because . . . because . . .

Today is your birthday!